THE WAY HOME FOR WOLF

For Baby Sky, who made it here to us through the
blanket of stars. We love you so much — R B

For Jodie, James, Rafe and Wilf — J F

ORCHARD BOOKS
First published in Great Britain in 2018
by The Watts Publishing Group

1 3 5 7 9 10 8 6 4 2

Text © Rachel Bright, 2018
Illustrations © Jim Field, 2018

A CIP catalogue record for this book is available from the British Library

978 1 40834 920 5

Printed and bound in China

FSC
www.fsc.org

MIX
Paper from
responsible sources
FSC® C104740

Orchard Books, an imprint of Hachette Children's Group
Part of The Watts Publishing Group Limited
Carmelite House,
50 Victoria Embankment,
London EC4Y 0DZ
An Hachette UK Company
www.hachette.co.uk
www.hachettechildrens.co.uk

Rachel
BRIGHT

Jim
FIELD

THE WAY HOME FOR
WOLF

ORCHARD

Dusting diamonds of ice in a desert of white,
The wild, whipping wind, it whistled its tune
To a howling of wolves and a shimmering moon.

And the loudest "ARrrroooOOO" in this echoing song
Was a wolfling called Wilf at the heart of the throng.
He loved to be fierce and longed to be grown.
He liked to try everything **ALL ON HIS OWN.**

"Look at me! I am big!
I am tough!" he would growl,

whilst he showed
off his strength

and practised his prowl.

One night it was time for the wolves to move on . . .
New folks had moved in and their shelter was gone!
So they left right away, to find a new cave.
They would have to walk far and they'd have to be brave.

"Let's go!" shouted Wilf, "I am ready to LEAD."

"You're too small," laughed the wolves, "it's an elder we need."

"One day," they advised, "you will guide from the front."

"I suppose," muttered Wilf with a huff and a grunt.

They struggled through snow as high as their flanks

And leapt over rocks as they scaled icy banks

Wilf gave his all to keep pace and keep up,
But strong-willed as he was, he was still just a pup.

He kept dropping
back with each clamber
and climb,

as the pack journeyed
further away all the time.

Exhausted and breathless,
he strayed off the track

when a blizzard blew in . . .

. . . and he lost his way back.

Wilf longed to howl, "Help!"
and to holler it loud . . .
But his throat was too hoarse
and his heart was too proud.

He lay on the tundra,
his tail curled up tight.
A blanket of stars was
his bed for the night.
Until . . .

CRACK!
went the ice.
CRACK
and
KER-EEEEAK!

Wilf jumped to all fours
with a deafening shriek.

He stuck out the
claws on every limb.
He **HAD** to hold on . . .
because Wilflings can't swim!

Then he fell and he fell,
rolling and spinning.

It felt like the end,
but was just the beginning . . .

. . . since somebody down there had heeded his scream
And she swooped from beneath like a watery dream.
"I'll help you!" she called. "Just reach for my horn!"
A majestic and magical . . . SEA UNICORN!

Wilf's pride washed away and he stretched out a paw
As she lifted him gently back onto the shore.

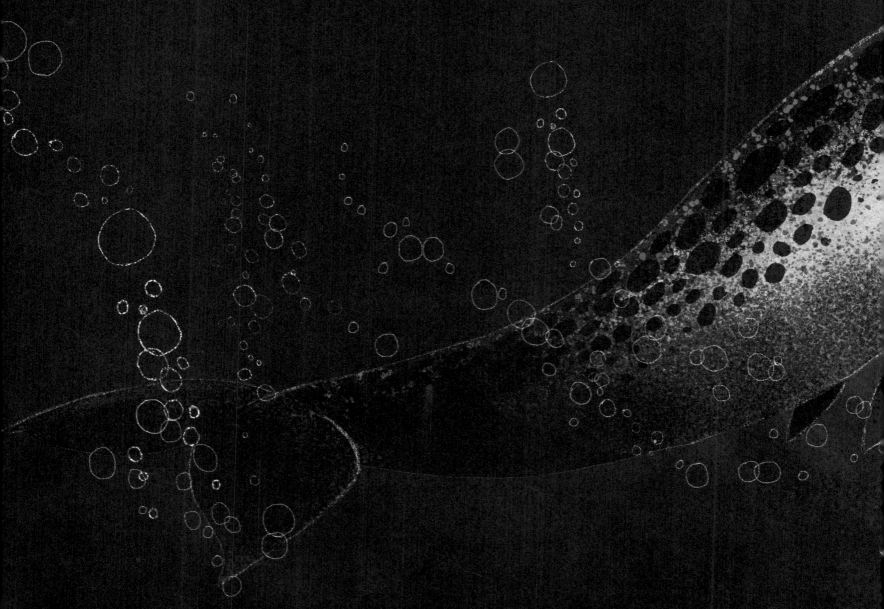

"Don't worry!" she sung
before dipping her brow,
"My friend MR WALRUS
will help you out now."

And there, right behind him, a huge, tusky fellow
Lifted his whiskers and let out a BELLOW!
"To the ridge!" he proclaimed with his chin in the air.
"My friend, mighty MUSK-OX, will take you from there."

And with waftings of fish and a very loud snort
Their journey was made and their travel seemed short.

And there, sure enough,
on the ridge was the ox,
Who took Wilf as far
as his friend . . .

...ARCTIC FOX

Who followed his nose
through the trees to a ...

...GOOSE

Who guided him,
honking, to ...

. . . this ancient MOOSE!

The moose knew these wilds
like no other soul.
He was steady and true
in pursuit of their goal.

And as twilight closed in,
Moose sang out a call
To a flittering, fluttering,
tiny fluffball . . .

A **BEAR-MOTH!** who showed

Wilf the rest of the way

To the place where this

wolfling most wanted to stay.

"THANK YOU!" Wilf waved
as he rejoined his pack,
And the wolves howled with joy
that their Wilfling was back.

They huddled him in and cuddled him close
And fussed over which wolf had missed him the most.
Wilf, he knew then, that when **ALL** come together
The darkest of times are easy to weather.

So he bowed to the narwhal, ox, walrus and goose,

And vowed to the fox, and the moth, and the moose . . .

"If ever I meet one who's strayed off their track,

I'll help them along by guiding them back."

And true to his word, Wilf is different now,
And his world seems much smaller and warmer somehow.

Since wherever life takes you, wherever you roam

...we're all just a handful
of friendships from home.

This
Treasure Cove Story
belongs to

FOLLOW THE NINJA

A CENTUM BOOK 978-1-912396-21-4
Published in Great Britain by Centum Books Ltd.
This edition published 2018. 1 3 5 7 9 10 8 6 4 2

Centum Books Ltd, 20 Devon Square, Newton Abbot,
Devon, TQ12 2HR, UK.

www.centumbooksltd.co.uk | books@centumbooksltd.co.uk
CENTUM BOOKS Limited Reg.No. 07641486.

A CIP catalogue record for this book is available
from the British Library.

Printed in China.

A Treasure Cove Story

TEENAGE MUTANT NINJA TURTLES

FOLLOW THE NINJA!

Adapted by **Geof Smith**
Based on the teleplay '**Follow the Leader**' by **Eugene Son**
Illustrated by **Steve Lambe**

The Teenage Mutant Ninja Turtles were on patrol. They had been looking for mutagen containers all night, but they hadn't found any.

'I'm so bored,' Mikey whined.

'Let's take a break and do something fun,'
suggested Leo, the Turtles' leader.
'Awesome!' his brothers cheered.

'It's time for a training session!' Leo exclaimed.
'Aww,' Raph, Donnie and Mikey moaned. Ninja
exercises didn't sound like fun to them.

Leo had an idea
to make training exciting.
'We'll play King of the Mountain,'
he said, jumping to the top of Dragon
Gate. 'I'll stand up here and you
try to get past me using ninja skills.'

'Sounds great,' Raph said. He whispered a secret plan to Mikey and Donnie.

Mikey went first. He put on his headphones,
then flipped, spun, and danced right past Leo.
'Ninjas don't do that!' Leo protested.

Donnie calculated a sneaky way to throw
his ninja stars. They bounced and skipped off
buildings – right towards Leo.

Leo ducked and when he looked up, Donnie
was behind him.

$$2ab+b^2$$

$$\frac{b}{a+b}$$

$$(a+b)^2$$

$$\frac{5x}{2}$$

Raph threw his *sai* straight at Leo.
As Leo dodged it, Raph jumped past him.
'That's not fair!' Leo shouted.

Leo was really angry. 'You guys never take my orders seriously.'
'Well, you always want us to fight just like you,' Raph replied
as he, Donnie and Mikey marched away.

Back at the lair, Leo spoke to his teacher, Splinter. 'Maybe I'm not cut out to be a leader,' he said.

'A true ninja must
be unpredictable,'
Splinter said. 'And
a true leader doesn't
always tell his
followers what to do.

He must trust them
to grow on their own.'

The next night, the Turtles went out again. Suddenly, Karai jumped from the shadows. She was a very dangerous ninja – and she wasn't alone. An army of ninja robots stood behind her!

'My Footbots are programmed to know every ninja move,' she said. 'You can't beat them!'

Karai commanded the Footbots to capture the Turtles. The bots charged and the battle began. The Footbots ducked the Turtles' punches. They blocked the Turtles' kicks. The Turtles couldn't stop them!

Leo was sure the Turtles would lose this fight...
until he remembered Splinter's words: *A true ninja
must be unpredictable.*

'You can't program a ninja,' Leo said. Then he yelled to his brothers. 'Do you remember King of the Mountain? Show these bots your original ninja moves!'

The Footbots weren't programmed to deal with
Mikey's dancing.
 Donnie was too sneaky for them.
 And Raph's power put the bots on the run!

$$\frac{b}{a+b}$$

'That's the most fun I've ever had following your orders!' Raph exclaimed.

'That's the most fun I've had giving them,' Leo replied.

Mikey threw a smoke bomb,
and the Turtles vanished into
a purple cloud.

Back at their lair, the Turtles were ready to relax.
'Who wants to play King of the Mountain?' Leo
joked.
'I'd rather play Follow the Leader,' Raph said with
a smile.

Treasure Cove Stories

Book list may be subject to change.

An ongoing series to collect and enjoy!